LFO

backstage pass

by Kimberly Walsh

DEVIN

BRAD

RICH

adidas

SCHOLASTIC INC.

New York   Toronto   London   Auckland   Sydney
Mexico City   New Delhi   Hong Kong

Photo Credits

Front Cover: Ann Bogart;   Back Cover: Joseph Galea;   1: Ann Bogart;   2: Ann Bogart;   3: Joseph Galea;   4: Joseph Galea;   5 (both): Jon McKee/Retna Limited, USA;   6 (both): Jon McKee/Retna Limited, USA;   7: Joseph Galea;   8 (both): Bill Davila/Retna Limited, USA;   9 (all): Bill Davila/Retna Limited, USA;   10 (both): Bill Davila/Retna Limited, USA;   11 (top): Bill Davila/Retna Limited, USA;   11 (bottom left): Bill Davila/Retna Limited, USA;   11 (bottom right): Joseph Galea;   12: Ann Bogart;   13 (top): Bill Davila/Retna Limited, USA;   13 (bottom): Joseph Galea;   14 (left): Barry Talesnick/Retna Limited, USA;   14 (right): Celebrity Photo Agency Inc.;   15 (both): Joseph Galea;   16-17: Ann Bogart;   18: Joseph Galea;   19 (top): Joseph Galea;   19 (bottom left): Barry Talesnick/Retna Limited, USA;   19 (bottom right): Joseph Galea;   20: Joseph Galea;   21 (top): Joseph Galea;   21 (bottom): Ann Bogart;   22-23: Ann Bogart;   24-25: Ann Bogart;   26: Joseph Galea;   27 (top): Ann Bogart;   27 (bottom left): Joseph Galea;   27 (bottom right): Ann Bogart;   28 (top): Joseph Galea;   28 (bottom): Mitch Gerber/Corbis;   29: Bill Davila/Retna Limited, USA;   30-31: Ann Bogart;   32-33 (top right): Robert Domingo;   32-33 (bottom, far left): Paul Fenton/Shooting Star;   32-33 (bottom, second from left): Robert Domingo;   34: Ann Bogart;   35 (all): Joseph Galea;   36: Ann Bogart;   37: Joseph Galea;   38: Ann Bogart;   39 (top): Bill Davila/Retna Limited, USA;   39 (bottom): Joseph Galea;   40: Bill Davila/Retna Limited, USA;   41: Joseph Galea;   42 (top): Ann Bogart;   42 (bottom both): Joseph Galea;   43 (top): Barry Talesnick/Retna Limited, USA;   43 (bottom): Ann Bogart;   44 (top left): Joseph Galea;   44 (top right): Ann Bogart;   44 (bottom): Joseph Galea;   45 (top): Jon McKee/Retna Limited, USA;   45 (bottom): Bill Davila/Retna Limited, USA;   46: Joseph Galea;   47 (top): Joseph Galea;   47 (bottom): Ann Bogart;   48: Joseph Galea

ISBN 0-439-15967-9

12 11 10 9 8 7 6 5 4 3 2 1   9/9 0 1 2 3 4/0

Printed in the U.S.A.

First Scholastic printing, October 1999

RICH   BRAD   DEVIN

Contents

Guide To What's Inside

RICH

DEVIN

BRAD

**The original LFO —
Brad, Rich,
and Brian.**

Introduction

The Legend

Once upon a time, the Motown Sound ruled pop and soul music. Legendary bands, like the Four Tops, Temptations, Jackson 5, and the Supremes had hit after hit. They called it Motown because Detroit, where all these groups were formed, is also known as the Motor City. [Think: cars are made there.]

Okay, enough history. 'Cause *that*, bay-bay, bay-bay, was THEN.

THIS is NOW.

And circa now, the place for the purest pop on the planet is coming from O-TOWN! The O stands for Orlando — that's in Florida, of course — and the musicians bringin' it to ya are Backstreet Boys, 'N Sync, Britney Spears, Christina Aguilera, C-Note, Take Five . . . and . . . three totally talented dudes named Rich, Brad, and Devin: LFO!

That said, the LFO story actually started far away from O-Town. It started even before these gold 'n' platinum performers hit the music charts' top digits.

While millions of tourists flocked to the sun-drenched theme parks of Orlando, the roots of LFO were sprouting in West Roxbury and Dorchester, inner-city sections of cold and blustery Boston, Massachusetts.

The Cast

Rich Cronin hails from West Roxbury. Music was his first love, and, even as a kid, he was always writing songs. Melodies and lyrics seemed to flow from him. Back in the late 1980s his favorite group was New Edition, and he was practically hypnotized by their classic R&B harmonies. By the time he hit junior high, Rich had discovered rap, and was practicing his freestylin' in front of his bedroom mirror. He listened to everything, from old school masters like the Sugar Hill Gang to newcomers like LL Cool J and Public Enemy.

Meanwhile, on the other side of Boston, **Brian Gillis** was exposed to a music phenomenon in his Dorchester neighborhood — the New Kids on the Block. A natural-born performer, Brian was not only inspired by, but also encouraged by New Kids' Danny Wood and Donnie Wahlberg. All three hung out at the local community center, the Dorchester Youth Collaborative, a haven from the mean streets of Dorchester. Before long, Brian was forming his own groups. For him, there was never ever anything else — rap was it!

The booming Boston music scene was producing hitmakers, one after another. Established rock and rollers like Aerosmith . . . pop heartthrobs like New Kids . . . funky ska groups like the Mighty Mighty Bosstones . . . and master rapper/composer Guru of Gang Starr all shared the local Boston club stages. It was in this mix that Rich and Brian met, liked each other's musical styles, and knocked around the idea of starting a duo.

A Group Is Born

By this time, Orlando, Florida — O-Town — was Pop Central, USA — mainly because of a businessman named Louis J. Pearlman. He financially backed and helped develop the Backstreet Boys and 'N Sync from the get-go. So Rich and Brian decided to go right to the source, and — armed with demos and videos of their songs — flew down to Orlando to scope out the scene. That's when **Brad Fischetti** came into the picture.

New York-born and New Jersey-bred, Brad had his own musical goals. Immersing himself in everything from R&B to hip-hop, Brad was always first to pick up the new CDs by favorites LL Cool J and the Beastie Boys. But he also had an ear for interesting new styles, and in 1997 he met Rich and Brian in Orlando. The three began talking music, and a few days later, began to fool around with some songs. Things clicked instantly.

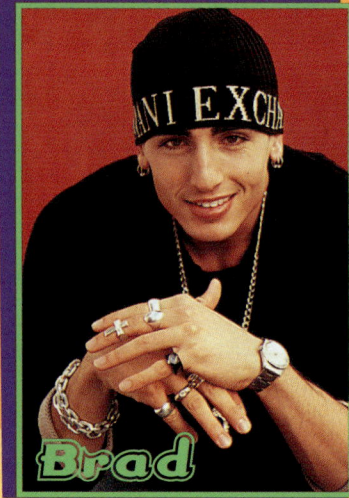

Rich, Brad, and Brian were all in their early twenties and each towered over the six-foot mark. Not only did their musical styles and tastes mesh, but they also *looked* like a group. They knew it was time to make it official. They considered all sorts of names, but settled on LFO, which stood for Lyte Funkie Ones. That's what Rich was called when he first started performing in public back in junior high.

Just days into their Florida adventure, they decided to make a bold move. They showed up at the front door of Lou Pearlman's Orlando estate! And this is where the magic comes in. First of all, Lou, who has been nicknamed "Big Poppa" by his groups, answered the door, and instead of calling security to escort these three young strangers off his property, actually listened to them and their music. He was so impressed he told them he'd work with them right then and there!

Growing Pains

That meant following the same formula that had worked for Backstreet Boys and 'N Sync — starting off in Europe. LFO signed with BMG Records in Germany, and hooked up with the (late) producer Denniz Pop, who had "platinumized" 'N Sync, BSB, ABBA, and Robyn. The plan worked. LFO's first two singles "The Way You Like It" and "Can't Have You," made a major buzz in Europe and Canada, and caught the attention of Clive Davis, the way famous and powerful head of BMG's Arista Records in the U.S.

However, as some major moves were about to happen — read: Arista Records signing LFO — Rich, Brad, and Brian were going through some changes. As each one wrote song after song, they soon realized that Rich and Brad were drifting more toward a pop, harmonic sound, and Brian was, at heart and soul, a rapper.

With no hard feelings, they decided to split up. Brian signed as a solo rap act — Mista Brizz — with Lou's company, while Rich and Brad searched for a third member. Then, Rich remembered hearing about a young singer back home in Boston. His name was **Devin**, and he could really wail. When Devin boarded the plane in Boston to fly down to Orlando, he had no idea what was in store for him. But it took about — oh, two seconds! — after the three sang together for the first time for everyone in the room to realize they had witnessed something ultra-special.

And in May 1999, when "Summer Girls" first hit the radio, the rest of the world knew it too.

BRAD

DEVIN

RICH

The "Summer Girls" Video
Join the LFO Beach Party!

Devin, Rich, and Brad take a break while the video crew sets up the next shot.

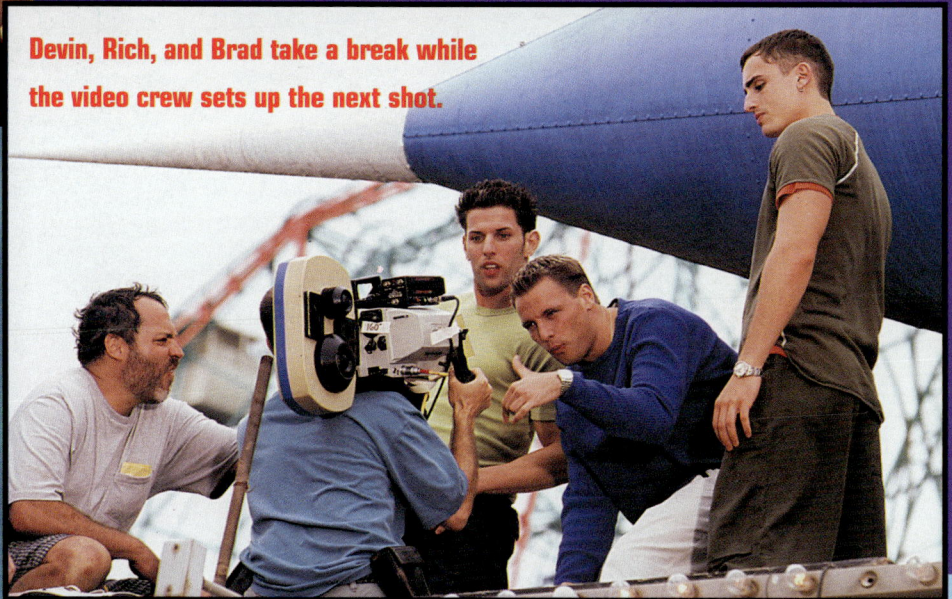

Brad, Rich, and Devin check out the beach scene at Coney Island.

Are you LFO's "Abercrombie & Fitch" girl?

Some might like it "under the boardwalk," but LFO prefers it up on the roof! The boardwalk fast food stands were a perfect *Summer Girls* location.

LFO could have filmed their debut video, *Summer Girls*, on the beaches of California or Florida, but instead, they chose the legendary home of "summer girls" — the beaches and boardwalk of Brooklyn, New York's Coney Island neighborhood. Classic summer songs like "Itsy Bitsy Teenie Weenie Yellow Polka Dot Bikini" and "Under the Boardwalk" were about fun-in-the-sun, and set in Coney Island, the original home of Nathan's Hot Dogs, the Cyclone Roller Coaster, and summer romances. Needless to say, when Rich, Brad, Devin, and the LFO video crew took over a small stretch of Coney Island, word spread like wildfire. Pretty soon, the boys were surrounded by hundreds of girls, all wishing they could star in their own, up-close-and-personal LFO video!

"You're the best girl I ever did see," sings Brad.

Hmmm, could Brad, Rich, and Devin be thinking about adding a fourth member to LFO?

Brad, Rich, and Devin with "Big Poppa" Lou Pearlman.

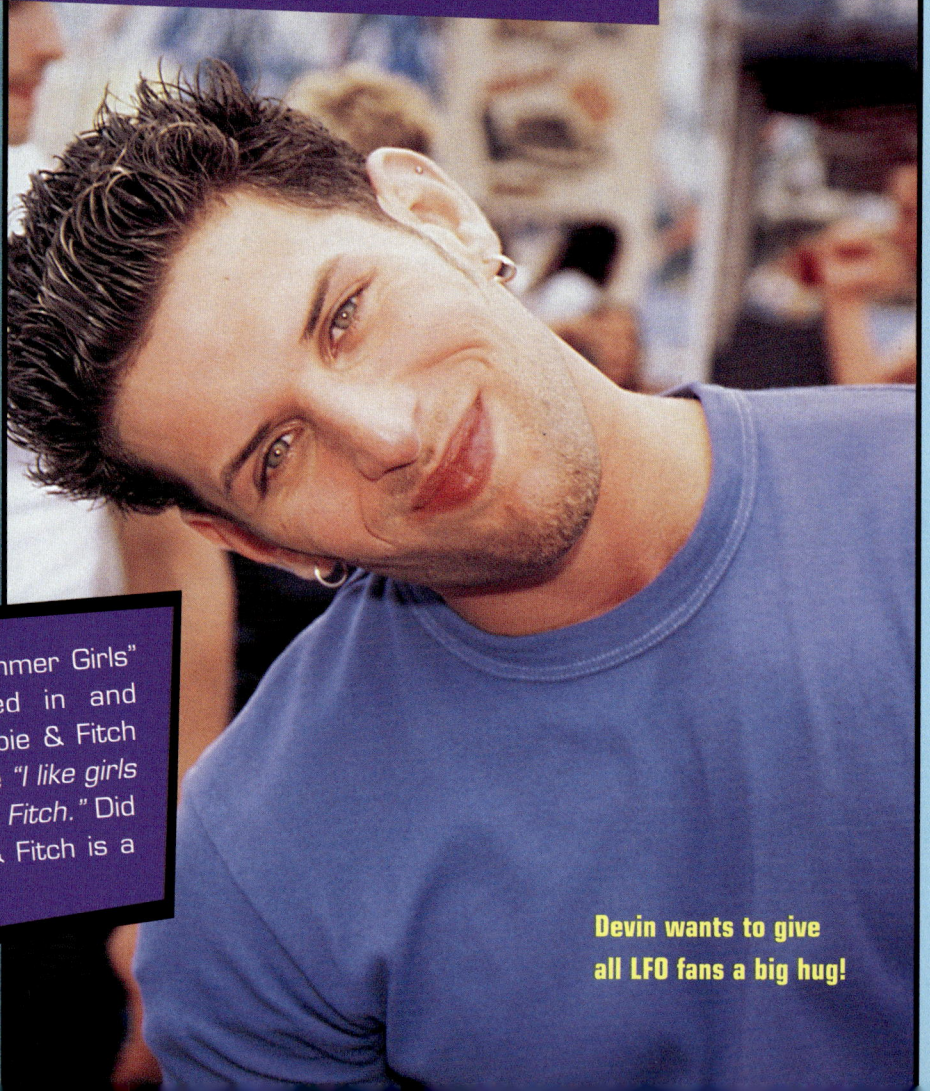

Fun Fact

When fans first heard "Summer Girls" on the radio, they called in and requested "that Abercrombie & Fitch song," because of lines like *"I like girls that wear Abercrombie & Fitch."* Did you know Abercrombie & Fitch is a clothing store?

Devin wants to give all LFO fans a big hug!

Rich thinks about all that has happened to LFO in the past few months. "It's incredible," he says.

LFO

Rich Cronin

Rich Cronin Sigh Guy!

"I grew up in West Roxbury on the south side of Boston — it was great," begins Rich Cronin at a press conference interview. A room full of eager reporters, each pressing their tape recorders in his face, don't seem to faze this young singer/songwriter. At first the writers are tempted to describe him with terms like "hunk," "babe," and "cutie." Though his blond spiked hair, easy grin, and sculpted body all scream "easy boy-band member," there's a lot more to this blond, green-eyed founding member of LFO.

Rich is intelligent, talented, and has a mischievous gift for a spur-of-the-moment, free-style rap — or giving friends "to-a-T" nicknames. In his heavy Boston accent, Rich wins over even the most skeptical of audiences. When he talks to you, he makes you feel like you are the most important person in the world. You soon realize there's going to be a laugh at the end of every one of his stories.

13

Rich attributes those qualities to his upbringing. "It was great," he explains. "I wasn't street or anything like that. Just regular. I had a lot of good friends. I went to parochial school, and the [nuns] kept me in check. The [nuns]! They were tough."

Though music was always Rich's first love, his parents, Doris and Richard, were determined that he get a good education. "I guess that's one of the reasons I got sent to parochial school. My father [insisted on that]. . . . I had a hard time in school. I was all right, but school didn't come easily to me. It was hard for me to pay attention. I was good at English and reading, but I had a hard time with math, so it made school a real struggle. I had to get a lot of extra help, like tutors. I got frustrated a lot."

Rich worked hard and made his family proud. He even got accepted to Bridgewater State College and majored in marketing. But in the

Rich is a great guitar player — and he jokes that he dabbles on the kazoo!

middle of his junior year, Rich had to make a decision: school or music. Music won out — and his family supported him completely.

It wasn't easy. Local fame, even if it is in Boston, doesn't guarantee bills being paid. Rich had to sacrifice a lot to follow his dream. But the day he first heard fans call in to a radio station and request "Summer Girls," he knew it was all worth it!

If Rich could meet just one celebrity, it would be Al Pacino. "He's such a cool actor," says Rich. Hmmm, maybe one day they'll co-star in a movie. It's possible!

Rich's Stat Sheet

Name: Richard Burton Cronin

Birth Date: August 30, 1975

Zodiac Sign: Virgo

Birthplace: Boston, MA

Current Home: Orlando, FL

Hair: Dirty Blond

Eyes: Green

Height: 6' 3"

Weight: 185 pounds

Parents: Richard and Doris Cronin

Brother: Mike

Sister: Cassie

High School: Sacred Heart High School, Boston, MA

College: Bridgewater State (2½ years)

Heritage: Irish, English, Swedish

Righty or Lefty: Right-handed

Innie or Outtie: Innie

Boxers or Briefs: Boxers

Shoe Size: 12

Hobbies: Going to the movies

Tattoos: None

Piercings: Ears

Favorites

Cartoon: Smurfs
Color: Green
Animal: Dog
Sport: Baseball
Sports Team: Boston Red Sox
Car: Jeep Wrangler
Food: Meatball sandwiches
Fast Food: Pizza
Candy: Twix
Ice Cream: Chocolate chip
Drink: Mountain Dew
Book: *Different Seasons* by Stephen King
TV Show: *Party of Five*
Movies: *Braveheart, Good Will Hunting*
Song: New Edition's "If It Isn't Love"
Singers: Jay-Z, Wyclef Jean
School Subject: English
Video Game: Pitfall
Cologne: Tommy Hilfiger
Toothpaste: Mentadent

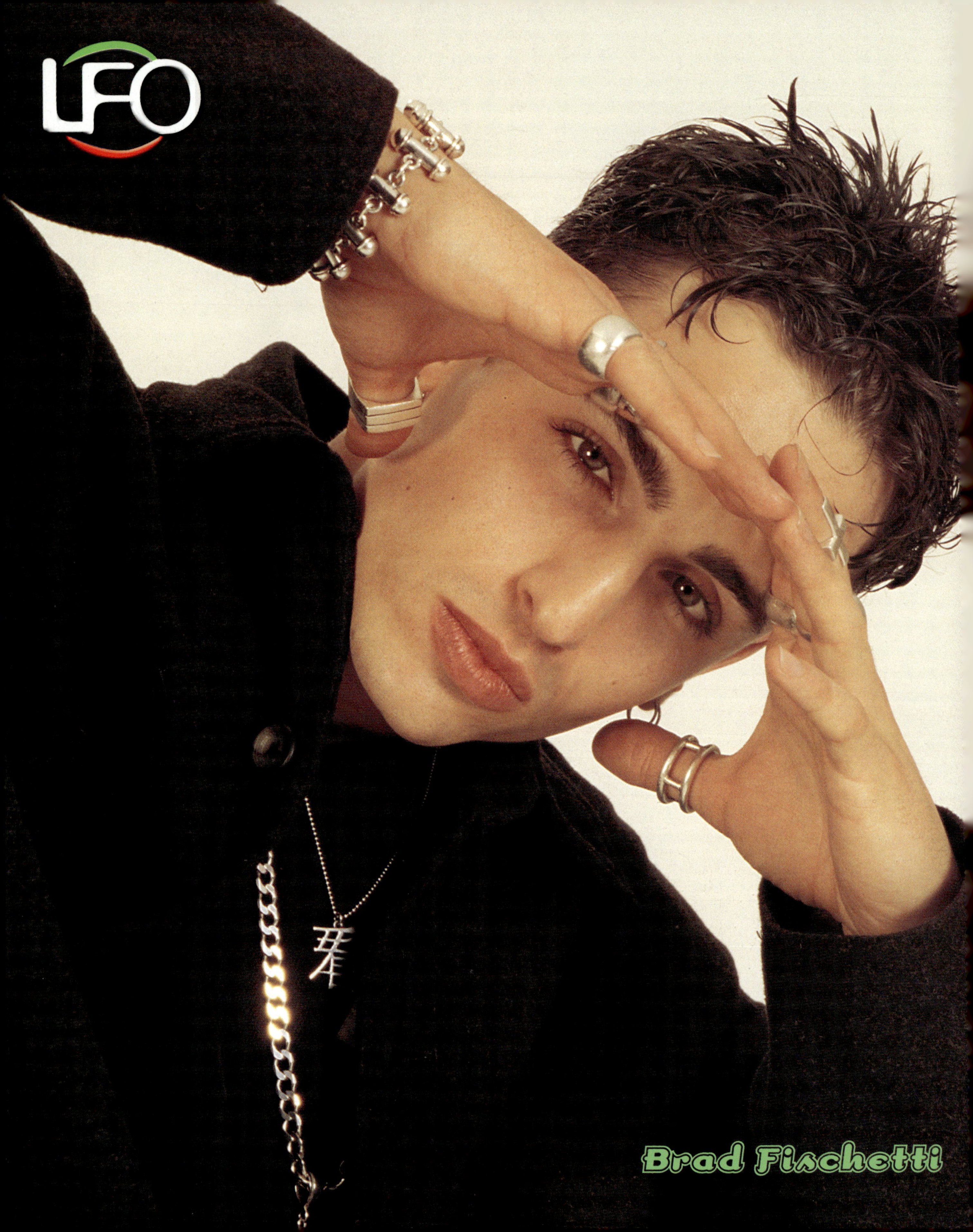
Brad Fischetti

Brad Fischetti Tuff Love!

Brad Fischetti agrees with Rich that the LFO road to success wasn't always smooth riding. There were bumps along the way, but this New York-born, New Jersey-raised singer always was able to see the light at the end of the tunnel — even if sometimes it was only a glimmer.

"I first knew we clicked when we kept rocking shows," the ultimate tall, dark, and handsome heartthrob says. "No one knew who we were, but everyone loved our shows. I saw all those hours and hours of rehearsals really brought a chemistry to us on stage. We really had something there."

LFO takes a break — whew!

Wanna get Brad in a good mood? "Easy," he says. "Smile and be nice to me."

When asked whom he most admires, Brad says, "Will Smith. He's crossed boundaries in color, class, and field of work."

While Rich may be the laugh track of LFO, Brad is the soul. At first he seems serious, and perhaps a bit moody, but actually Brad is usually just internally analyzing things. He doesn't make snap decisions, and considers all possibilities. He says if he wasn't singing, "I'd be a personal trainer and nutritionist." But you know no matter how health-conscious Brad is, there was never any question he wouldn't pursue a career in music.

A firm believer in the power of positive thinking, Brad was sure LFO was going to make it. In their first incarnation — with Brian — they practically caused Beatle-like riots over in Germany. "People in Europe really supported us," Brad recalls of those early days. "People would say, 'The crowd doesn't even know who you are, but it's like they want you to be successful.' They were going crazy! I've got tapes. I'm on stage and I look out to fifty or sixty thousand people clapping. It's like a high to watch that. It's a crazy feeling."

When LFO returned from Europe, and underwent their personnel changes, Brad wasn't disheartened at the thought of having to start all over again with a new member. He knew LFO just had to keep their collective eye on their ultimate goal. He was right, and you've got to believe him when he tells you that "Summer Girls" is just the tip of the LFO iceberg!

"We're like brothers," explains Brad of the LFO relationship.

21

Brad's Stat Sheet

Name: Bradley David Fischetti

Nickname: Brad

Birth Date: September 11, 1975

Zodiac Sign: Virgo

Birthplace: New York, NY

Current Home: Orlando, FL

Hair: Brown

Eyes: Brown

Height: 6' 3"

Weight: 190 pounds

Parents: Susan Mauro and Richard Fischetti

Brothers: Michael, Bobby, and Richie

High School: Mahwah High School

College: University of Northern Texas (2 years)

Heritage: Italian, German, Irish

Righty or Lefty: Right-handed

Innie or Outtie: "Neither, just in the middle"

Boxers or Briefs: Boxer-briefs

Shoe Size: 12 or 13

Hobbies: Weight lifting, sleeping, writing

Tattoos: None

Piercings: 4 ear piercings

Cartoon: Beavis and Butthead

Color: Black

Animal: Cat

Sport: Baseball

Sports Teams: NY Mets, NY Yankees, NY Knicks, Miami Dolphins

Car: Lincoln Navigator

Foods: Pizza, Ice cream

Fruit: Grapefruit

Fast Food: Chick Fil-A grilled chicken sandwich

Candy: M&M's

Ice Cream: Rocky Road

Drinks: H_2O, Dr Pepper

TV Shows: *All in the Family, M*A*S*H, Fresh Prince of Bel Air*

Movies: *Romeo + Juliet, Top Gun, The Shawshank Redemption*

Song: Silk's "Lose Control"

School Subject: Gym

Video Game: NHL for Sega

Cologne: Tommy Hilfiger

Toothpaste: Crest

Devin
Definitely Delish!

Devin Lima — professionally he goes by the single name, Devin — grew up in New Bedford, MA, outside of Boston. Like his LFO mates, Brad and Rich, Devin's family was tight-knit and very supportive of each other. He's the oldest of three boys. "It's cool," Devin says. "We are close."

There was always music in the Lima household, and Devin pictured himself entertaining in front of an audience as far back as he can remember. By the time Devin was a sophomore

Hey, where are all the girls? Rich, Devin, and Brad check out the scene from the Coney Island boardwalk.

in high school, he says, "I became serious about music. I didn't have time for anything else."

His single-minded interest set Devin apart from the rest of his classmates. Of course, it didn't help that by nature Devin is something of a loner. "I was quiet," he admits. "I just watched."

By the time Devin had finished high school, he had hooked up with a local Boston music manager and began making the rounds of talent shows and club dates. His multi-octave voice could pull an audience to their feet halfway through a song. As with Rich, Devin became a familiar face on the local Boston music scene, but he always seemed half a handshake away from a record deal. A number of times he came very close to signing a contract with a record label as a solo act, but something always happened.

Devin wasn't one to give up. He plugged away. His life was still all about music. He worked a regular job,

Devin's roots are also Boston-deep. He credits one of the members of Marky Mark's Funky Bunch with teaching him his dance moves!

but then he went to rehearsals or local shows. The LFO offer was just the break he needed.

"I had known Devin from Boston through a friend who's his manager," Rich told *Teen Beat* magazine. "When he heard we needed a new guy, he said, 'Hey, how 'bout Devin?' So, [Devin] flew down to Orlando and me, him, and Brad hit if off really big and we liked the way he sounded. It worked."

Though it was a bit of a whirlwind for Devin, after a few months it was as if he had been with LFO all along. Yet, even then, Devin was surprised at the turn of events. "Months ago, what was I doing?" he explained at a press conference. "I was in Boston, working forty hours a week, going to the gym, and singing all day. I thought I was content with that because I assumed one day it would happen. Then I started realizing, I'm getting better and better, with no way to show it. My room was my audience — I had to move on up."

And move on up Devin did. His soulful voice was the perfect complement to Rich and Brad's. When Devin hits those notes, you feel something special deep down inside, and you just know he is the heart of LFO.

Devin describes himself as "funny, determined, and childish." Awwww!

Devin's Stat Sheet

Name: Harold Devin Lima
Nickname: Devin
Birth Date: March 18, 1977
Zodiac Sign: Pisces
Birthplace: Boston, MA
Current Home: Orlando, FL
Hair: Brown
Eyes: Green
Height: 5' 11"
Weight: 184 pounds
Parents: Louis and Filomena Lima
Brothers: Derek, Nick
High School: New Bedford High School
Heritage: Portuguese
Righty or Lefty: Right-handed
Innie or Outtie: Innie
Boxers or Briefs: Boxers
Shoe Size: 12
Hobbies: Drawing, singing, working out
Tattoos: A cross and a dragon
Piercings: Ears
Early Musical Influences: "I remember listening to Cinderella and Def Leppard."

Harold (Devin) Lima

Cartoon: Batman

Color: Green

Animal: Cheetah

Sport: Football

Car: Lamborghini

Food: Chicken, cereal, peanut butter and jelly sandwiches

Fast Food: Subway

Candy: Sour Patch Kids

Ice Cream: None — yogurt

Drink: Water

TV Shows: *Batman*, *Superman* cartoons

Movies: *Braveheart*, *Star Wars*

Fashion Designer: Calvin Klein

Singers: Boyz II Men, Jodeci, Stevie Wonder

Book: *Wuthering Heights* — "It made me realize you can keep on loving one girl forever."

School Subjects: Science and math

Video Game: President Evil for PlayStation

Cologne: Gillette

"The best thing about performing is just being able to let yourself go on stage," says Brad. "You can go wild. Sometimes I don't even remember being on stage. I come off and I'm like 'Wow that was crazy!'"

LFO became the most popular pop group on New York City's Z100 radio station — whenever they're in town, they stop by for a visit.

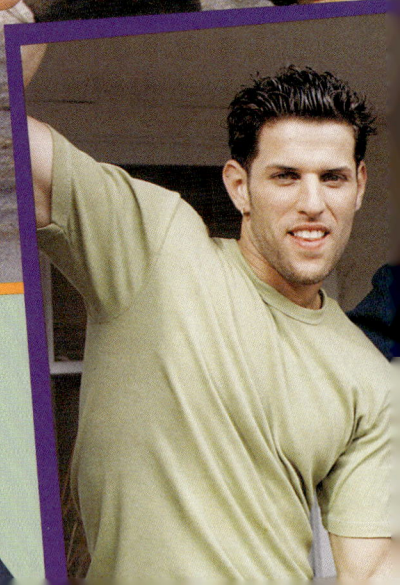

Just Chillin' With LFO

The guys performed at the farewell party for Z100 dj, Elliot.

Splish splash — LFO and friends take a summer dip!

33

Made You Blush!
LFO Confession-Session

34

On stage, Rich, Brad, and Devin are the ultimate cool ones. They can have a party with a free-style rap that makes everyone laugh, and they can sing a love ballad that touches every heart in the house. They have it all under control . . . but, like everyone else in the world, they have had their embarrassing moments. Check 'em out!

Rich — Counted Out!
"My most embarrassing moment? It had to be when I realized there wasn't a seat for me at my own high school graduation!"

Brad — Out For The Count!
"Back in eighth grade we used to play this game, 'Two for Flinching.' One of your friends would go like this [throw a fake

Brad believes the only thing that keeps a relationship alive is "trust."

Devin wants to meet a girl who "will believe in me."

Rich says the most important quality in a girlfriend is "honesty."

35

punch], and if you flinched, they got to hit you two times. One time I turned around in science class, and this guy was trying to play the 'Two for Flinching' game. He accidentally punched me in the nose. It was right after [the class had] watched some movie about death, so I thought I was dying. He didn't do it on purpose, but he got in trouble. They took me away in a wheelchair to the nurse. My mom had to come home from work. I thought she'd be compassionate, but she was like, 'Get over here! Let's go home!' I was like, 'Mom, I just got punched in the nose!'"

Devin — Lost Count

"When was I most embarrassed? I guess it was when I was singing at my junior year class banquet, and I forgot the lyrics. I just kept repeating the same line."

Goofin' With Regis & Kathie Lee

During an amazing appearance on TV's *Regis and Kathie Lee*, LFO performed "Summer Girls," and then sat down for a quick chat. Naturally, the boys were asked exactly what LFO stands for. Rich quipped, "It has stood for a bunch of different things, but now we just like the way the initials look together!"

BRAD

RICH

DEVIN

LFO on . . . Girls! Girls! Girls!

Rich on Career vs. Relationship:

"I figure [LFO] is my dream, and if I compromise this for a girl, that's not right. I think Brad Pitt said, if you really love someone, you're not going to have to compromise anything, it's just going to happen. I don't know. Sometimes I wonder, maybe I am missing out, maybe I'm never going to have that girl or anything. But if it's meant to be, it's meant to be."

Brad on Ms Right:

"I really don't have a particular type. As long as she treats me right and she's nice, that's the most important thing."

Rich on Ms Right:

"I don't know what I look for. I see gorgeous girls with nice personalities every day, and I don't necessarily think, Well, maybe I'd like to date her because she's cute or she's funny. All those things are important to me. But when I meet someone I want to date for real, there's this vibe I get. Like I see her, and there's something different about her — I want to get to know her."

Turn-ons	Turnoffs
Devin: "Girls with cute feet"	"Girls who wear too much makeup"
Brad: "Pretty feet"	"Smoking"
Rich: "Her eyes and her smile"	"Negativity"

Devin on Ms Right

"I'd like to have a girl who looks at me [with love]. But what do I do? Do I [concentrate] on my music? I don't have a guarantee; I don't know what's really going to come out of it. But I'm putting one hundred percent into it. Right now I have to put that one hundred percent into music rather than into someone else . . . . I have plenty of time to worry about [relationships] . . . . But when I do have a relationship, the girl has to believe in me."

Devin on His Most Romantic Date:

"It was when I was with this girl at the beach and we kissed while the tide crashed on us."

Brad on His Most Romantic Date:

"We walked through the woods and ended it with a kiss."

Rich on His Most Romantic Date:

"We were on the beach at Cape Cod."

Do you like it when a girl asks you out?

Rich: "Yes!!! I love that."

Devin: "That would be different for a change."

Brad: "Sure. I'm shy sometimes."

Rich on His Worst Date:

"I was dating a girl, [Miss X — for anonymity] in Orlando. . . . But because I was on the road [a lot], I didn't want a [steady] girlfriend right then. So she asked if she could see other people, and I said fine. Then one night, I took her to see *Titanic*, and when we were leaving the movie, A.J. from the Backstreet Boys was standing there outside the theater. I'm like, 'Hey, A.J., what's up?' And he's like, 'Actually I'm here for [Miss X]. She said after the movie with you, we were going out.' And then she said, 'You *said* I could see other people, baby!'"

Brad on His Worst Date:

"[Lately] I haven't gone on too many dates, but a few months ago, I had set one up with this girl. I was going on a real date, like, so I got dressed and I went to the store and picked up some flowers. I get into my car, and she calls and says, 'Can't do, sorry. There's a hurricane in Miami and my friends are flying up [to Orlando] to get away from the hurricane.' I was so mad, I hung up on her. She called me back and asked if we could meet a little later. I agreed and told her to call me up. No call. Then she called me a week later to apologize and ask to try again. So we tried again, but this time I didn't get dressed up or anything. . . . She *didn't* show up again!"

40

DEVIN   BRAD   RICH

Secret Stuff— a Peek in the LFO Diary!

Rich: The First Time I Ever . . .
Went to a Concert: Bell Biv Devoe
Bought an Album: Men at Work
Date: "In the sixth grade — we went bowling."
Kiss: "My first kiss was a disgusting horror show!"

Brad: The First Time I Ever . . .
Went to a Concert: R. Kelly/ Salt 'n' Pepa in 1994
Bought an Album: MC Hammer
Date: "Regina — we went to the roller rink. We were in fourth grade."
Kiss: "I was kissing girls in kindergarten. But my first real kiss was at a high school dance. I was dancing real close with this girl and after about a half hour I kissed her. I had no idea *what* I was doing."

Devin: The First Time I Ever . . .
Went to a Concert: Color Me Badd
Bought an Album: Jodeci
Date: "I can't remember!"
Kiss: "Lydia — in high school"

Peace and out — Devin!

A pensive Brad lost in his thought

Take a cruise with LFO — it will definitely be the "Love Boat."

42

Rich and singer Jessica Simpson met at a *Teen People* party.

Silly Tidbits

- **Brad** confesses he learned how to kiss by "practicing on a pillow. I was so scared. I was slobbering!"

- **Rich** laughs, "I used to practice [kissing] on the wall. I'd watch soap operas, and I'd be like, what are they doing? I don't get it!"

- **Devin** likes to do little, fun things to prove his love. "I was never a person to buy big gifts — I never had the money! But [there was one girl] — every day I used to write notes to her and draw her name. She loved bananas, so once I put a bunch of bananas in a box and gave them to her."

LFO's Secret Nicknames For Each Other

Devin: "Riff-asaurus Rex" because according to Brad and Rich, "He riffs a lot!"

Rich: "Rich Nice" — They gave it to me because I was always friendly."

Brad: "B From New Jersey"

Surprise! Surprise!

- **Brad:** "I have a rabbit as a pet. A little albino. I call him Dumpster Butt."

- **Rich:** "I'm really sensitive."

- **Devin:** "My hero is Arnold Schwarzenegger — everyone said he couldn't act, and he did!"

The first things that attract Rich to a summer girl — and a fall, winter, and spring girl — are her smile and her eyes.

Devin shows off
his tattoo.

Did you know that Brad plays the keyboard?

Rich, Brad, and Devin on What LFO Stands For

• It used to be for Lyte Funkie Ones, but the guys jokingly told Teen magazine it was "undergoing changes." Rich joked it stood for, "Larry, Frank, and Oscar, just 'cause it sounds funny." Brad joined in with his suggestion, "Live From Orlando, 'cause that's where we live now."

• **But the final decision was made** — now it's an anagram for their last names: **L** (Devin Lima)
F (Brad Fischetti)
O (O'Cronin, which was Rich's real family name when they first came to America from Ireland)

Let's hear it
for the boys!

44

Whatever Happened to Brian?   Meet Mista Brizz!

Former LFO member, Brian Gillis, now goes by the stage name Mista Brizz. Though he split with his former partners, it was very friendly, because Brizz wanted to go in another direction. Right now he's working hard perfecting his solo act, which features his unique style of pop, rap, and hip-hop. His party-hardy lyrics and dynamic stage show keeps things jumpin'. As his bio says, "Mista Brizz is the New Style, the New Flava. Mista Brizz is the new way of music."

Brian, now known as Mista Brizz, started his first group back in Boston with friends from the Dorchester Youth Collaborative, the same youth center the New Kids came from.

A week after Brad, Rich, and Devin shot *Summer Girls*, they appeared on *Live With Regis and Kathie Lee.*

45

Discography and Stuff

Debut CD: *LFO* (1999)
(as of publishing date)
First CD Single: "Summer Girls"
B-Side: "Can't Have You"

First Video: *Summer Girls*

Album Tracks (as of publishing date)
"The Girl on TV"
"Your Heart Is Safe With Me"
"I Don't Want to Kiss You Goodnight"
"I Will Show You Mine"
"All I Need to Know"
"Forever"
"Baby Be Mine"
"Summer Girls"
"Can't Have You"

Musical Notes

• Rich wrote and produced "Summer Girls" and "The Girl on TV"
• Multi award-winning songwriter Diane Warren wrote "Your Heart Is Safe With Me"
• Clive Davis was executive producer on the CD; Full Force and TQ were producers on several of the songs.
• LFO has opened for LL Cool J, Salt 'n' Pepa, and the Backstreet Boys, but in the fall of 1999 they began their own headlining tour.
• "Summer Girls" entered *Billboard*'s 100 Top Singles Chart as the "Hot Shot Debut."

The boys of "*Summer Girls*," are ready to riff, rap, and rock out big time. The success of that one song catapulted them onto the pop charts, and straight into fans' hearts. Now, they're ready to take on . . .

The road! While LFO has been making scattered promotional appearances all year long, they'll be headlining their own coast-to-coast tour starting this winter.

Single number two! Will the next single be as ultra-cool as "Summer Girls"? Well, duh. It'll be more than that, for while the song itself hasn't been selected, it'll prove that LFO can do ballads as well as they hip-hop.

Video mania! The *Summer Girls* video kicked it off and there's no question follow-up vids will be MTV heavy rotation-friendly.

A Disney Channel Concert Special! The band taped one of those cool Disney cable TV concerts — it airs by the end of the year.

"Fan-de-monium." LFO had true-blue fans before they even had a hit single, a fact that the boys will never forget.

Believe Brad when he promises that no matter what, they will remain the same down-to-earth, approachable guys they've always been. "We are trying to do this [the right way]," he insists. "A lot of groups change as they get successful. We just want to keep our feet on the ground . . ."

. . . and their songs in your hearts!

What's Next for LFO

Join the LFO bandwagon!